Trust Life

by
Barry Thomas Bechta

**UNCONDITIONAL
LOVE BOOKS**

*Redefining, Guiding, and Inspiring Humanity's
Connection to the Creative Power within.*

Trust Life
by
Barry Thomas Bechta

Library and Archives Canada Cataloguing in Publication

Bechta, Barry Thomas, 1968-
    Trust life / by Barry Thomas Bechta.

ISBN 978-0-9813485-1-3

    I. Title.

PS8603.E417T78 2009   **C813'.6**   **C2009-906530-4**

Publisher's Note
This publication is designed to provide accurate and authoritative information in regard to the subject matter covered. It is sold with the understanding that the author/publisher is not engaged in rendering psychological, legal, or other professional service. If advice or other assistance is required in those areas, the services of a competent professional should be sought.

Cover Photo By: Torvald Lekvam
http://torvald.lekvam.no

Trust Life

Part 1

I don't think that life is supposed to be like this. Really, is it supposed to be a struggle? Am I supposed to never have enough? Why do so many people around me seem to have more than I have? When will I ever have enough? What do I have to do God? Just tell me! Please I beg you to tell me! What have I done to deserve this? Am I not right in some way? I've done mostly good things. I've done some bad. Overall I am a good person. I really am a good person. Please help me!

Have you ever prayed? Really prayed as if your life depended upon it? As if you were never going to make it to tomorrow? Prayed with absolute faith and desperation? I mean prayed to a God you didn't fully believe in, but because of the pain you were feeling you hoped there was an outside chance? Prayed to a God whom never seemed to answer your prayers before, so why would it make a difference now? I have prayed that way. Today I am praying that way. But as I tell you this story it is not really today. Today was six months ago.

I have to get the kids up and going to school. Being a single mom isn't the easiest thing in the whole world. I get on. I have to get on. If I don't get on, nothing is going to get done.

My ex-husband, HA! That's a joke. He sees the kids maybe once every couple of months if they're lucky. Just because they are lucky to see him, doesn't mean I'm lucky they saw him.

It's like sending the kids to some kind of boot camp for candy. The kids come home miserable as sin. I doubt they get an hour's sleep all weekend. To top it off they are irritable as junkies

1

coming down from their latest sugar fix.

Who am I to complain? I get a weekend off, right? If you call Saturday morning at ten until Sunday at noon a weekend, boy do I have some swamp land I want to sell you.

Don't even get me started on the money thing. That son of a gun doesn't even pay his support payments. Alright. He paid a couple of times. He loves his kids. He really does. He's just not reliable. He says he's going to call the kids, and then he doesn't. He says he's going to pick the kids up from school, and I get a call at work telling me they're still at school. Why the hell doesn't it ever change?

Listen to me rant and rave. I haven't even got the kids out of bed yet.

I walk into the bedroom and shake my son gently on the shoulder, "Aaron."

Aaron is my ten year old son. Sweetest thing you are ever going to meet. He's like his father. In the good ways that is. He's funny and hard working and he really does everything he can to help around the house. If it weren't for Aaron, I don't know what I'd do. And he's good with Sarah.

"Sarah. Morning sweety." I kiss Sarah on the forehead.

Sarah is a little fireball. I wish she would settle down at night quicker. She wants to stay up later than me. I got to work early. Once she's asleep, it's great. She usually sleeps through until morning. There was some bed wetting for a while when her dad was first gone, but that seems to have stopped.

It's great when their dad picks them up one night a week. He's done that a couple of times. I've actually gone out on a couple of dates. I went out with some girl friends. I've even gone out with a few guys. Nothing serious. Just some fun. I never knew sex could be so fun again. I take all the necessary precautions. I'm safe. Don't you worry about me. I'm a big girl now, and I got this all under control.

I call the kids from the kitchen, "Aaron! Sarah! Up and at 'em!"

Aaron grumbles from under his sheets, "I'm up."

"Don't give me that." I say down the hall. "Get up both of you."

"I'm not feeling well." Sarah says from her side of the room.

"That's too bad. If I gotta go to work, by sonny Jesus in heaven, you gotta go to school."

"Mommy said a swear word." Aaron says.

"I'll tan your hide, if you're not out of bed by the count of three." I say from the kitchen. "One." I don't hear a thing. "Two." I say a little louder and then just as I am about to say *three*, I hear the crash of feet on the linoleum floor.

"We're up." they say together.

Sarah runs into the kitchen screaming, "Mommy! Mommy! Mommy!" This is something Sarah has done with me for years.

I don't drop them off at school. I go to work at seven thirty. I work at a coffee shop nearby. Aaron takes Sarah to school. We only live a few blocks away. I take the car and drive to work. This is my very first car. We had a family car when I was with my ex. I never even had my licence when I was with my ex. He liked to do

3

all the driving. He was less than stellar at it too. Me? I drive okay. I mean . . . I've not hit anyone. I was not saying that my ex did. He did, but I wasn't saying that.

I walk into the coffee shop. The bell on the top of the door clangs.

"Hello Martha."

That's me. I'm Martha. I didn't pick the name. My parents did. Don't get me started about that. I mean who names their kid Martha in the sixties. Seriously couldn't they have picked something cooler? No they couldn't. Wouldn't if they could. Bible belt, you know. That's where I grew up. You don't want to be named something like Freedom *in the Bible belt. I'm just glad they didn't name me Mary. They called my brothers John and Joseph. I'm lucky that my grandmother was called Martha, and that my daddy was so fond of her.*

"Hello Judy." I say.

Judy's my boss. She's a good boss. She lets me come and go when I need to with the kids and all. She's a no nonsense kid of woman. She's tough as nails. If I didn't know it, I'd swear she's always been the age she is now. I can't really imagine her being a kid, you know. When I think about it, I always picture just a shrunk down version of her.

"Morning Martha." Joe says.

Joe is Judy's husband. He does the cooking and cleaning. He's not very talkative. Judy does most of the talking for both of them. You know who's wearing the pants in their family. Joe's a good worker. He seems like a good man. He's always got a smile. I don't think he drinks too much. I've been married to worse. I wouldn't marry him, nothing like that. He's good and he's quiet.

4

I drop off my stuff under the counter and grab my apron hung on the wall. I grab a hot pot of coffee and start another one.

"Good morning, Mr. Jenkins. Refill?"

"Thank you."

Mr. Jenkins has been coming in here since the sixties. That's what Judy says. He and Mrs. Jenkins used to come in together. She's in a home now, so Mr. Jenkins comes in on his own.

I could tell you the story of everyone in here. Over in the corner booth is Sally. Sally is a few years younger than I am. She is, well how should I put this, Sally is a lady of the night. People make money all kinds of ways I reckon. Don't matter to me what she does. Lots of people in here talk as if it does matter. I suppose it could be a good way to make some money. I imagine it's probably pretty quick with some of the guys. I couldn't do it. I had enough trouble with my ex, I don't think I'd want to be doing it with most anyone.

Over there is Jack. Jack drives truck for some grocery company. He's in here three or four times a week. He's not married yet. He talks a good game though. I was thinking about it the other day. If he makes what he says he makes, I'm sure he's got a nice little nest egg set aside. Who knows, he might drink it away. Or spend it on the likes of Sally. Or maybe he's paying alimony for his own kids.

"Morning Jack." I motion with the coffee. "Do you have any kids?"

Jack smiles, "Why you ask?"

"I was just wondering."

"Sure I got a couple of kids and a couple of wives too."

"Seriously?"

"Seriously."

"You're putting me on."

"I had you, didn't I?"

"Yeah. You did. Can I get you anything else?"

"No. I'm just about ready to go."

I walk to the next table. "Morning Ethel."

Ethel has got to be in her eighties now. She doesn't look a day over sixty-five. She still lives in her house. Her husband is dead and gone over twenty years now. Town engineer he was. If you want to complain about the way some of the city hills are, he's the one to blame. That hill over on the south end of town, Washington Street, is a big pain come December. It'd be a far better road to toboggan down than to drive up. I think they must use over half the city budget for sand and salt each year on that hill alone. Ethel had nothing to do with that hill though. She definitely benefits from the pension her husband got for making that hill the way it is though. Lucky she has a daughter who still lives in town. Ethel's daughter, Rose, is a nice lady. I went to school with one of her kids. Although they were younger than me.

"Can you get me another one of those banana muffins, my dear?"

"Sure enough Ethel."

I pick the biggest, ripest, sweetest looking banana muffin for Ethel and I set it on a plate beside her.

"Can I get that to go." Ethel says.

Ethel always gets her banana muffin to go. I put it on the plate, because she enjoys the fun of it all. I remember one time, I just put the muffin in a bag on her table. She was grumpy as old heck when she left. Then Judy told me what's up. I never would have guessed that she has a beau at one of the senior centres. Judy says her mother is in the same centre and that Ethel goes in there each day. I imagine they talk in polite tones and laugh a little and perhaps even cry when they think of people whom have passed on.

"One banana muffin to go." I say with a smile and wait until she asks for her bill.

"Martha." Joe calls from the kitchen. "Order for table seven."

Table seven is the haunt of Jack Fisher. Everyone in the five surrounding counties knows Jack Fisher. Flew fighter planes in the second world war. I think he was in Korea too. People said he never came back the same.

I think anyone would come back different from a war. My Uncle Duane was in the war. He killed himself five years ago. I never knew him really well. My dad said he chose to go to Vietnam because he thought it was the right thing to do. I don't know if it was right or not, but I know he's gone now.

Jack Fisher is a quiet one. I think he'd just as soon disappear himself. He barely says a word, except to order his meal and he just says the number and thanks. That's about it.

The majority of people in the coffee shop come here every day. I maybe see a half dozen new people a week. We're not on a major thoroughfare. Once about twenty-five years ago, Jimmy Stewart even came into the coffee shop. The local newspaper reporter was following him about the town. That's why there is a picture of Jimmy with Joe and Judy above the alcove to the kitchen. Jimmy never signed it, on account of he was gone by the time the picture was developed, but it is an honest to goodness photo of the three of them, right here in the shop.

Judy's favourite movie is Rear Window. *I myself prefer* It's A Wonderful Life. *I like them both, but there is something about black and white movies. They just seem older, more classic like. I imagine what it'd be like with my very own guardian angel. I think it'd be great to know that someone always watches out for me.*

In the movie, Clarence is a pretty unlikely looking angel. I imagine that anyone could really be an angel with Clarence as an angel. Sometimes I even think that Arthur could be an angel.

"Morning Arthur."

I motion to fill his cup of coffee. Arthur places his hand over the open mouth of the cup.

"That's good."

"What if I poured hot coffee onto your hand when you did that?"

"I probably wouldn't give you a very good tip."

"You always give good tips."

"Don't tell the other waitresses, or they'll know I'm sweet on you."

Just then Veronica walks by, "You're only supposed to be sweet on me, Art."

"Just the two of you."

"What about me?" Judy calls over from the till.

"Admit it Arthur. You're just sweet."

"You've got me. I don't need any more sugar." He winks as he says sugar.

I playfully smack Arthur on the shoulder with my order pad. "You old smoothie."

"No more smoothies either." he says with a grimace across his face. "They give me gas." Then he laughs.

Arthur saved a woman from a car accident a few years ago. It was three in the morning one night. As he tells it, he just woke up and knew he had to drive down old Johnson Road. At three in the morning, he got dressed and drove down there. There was this lady who had crashed her car off the Johnson Road bridge. She was unconscious, and water was in her car. Luckily her head was above water. Arthur got her out of there and everything was okay. He got a key to the city for his actions. He was just glad he was there to help her out.

Now the cheapest son of gun in town is William Owens sitting in the next booth. I say cheap because he won a lottery ten months back. He won one of those big lotteries. You know big! I think the exact figure was just over six million. He has no family to speak of. He still lives in the same house. He drives the oldest pickup this side of Texas. And I also know for a fact, he is the stingiest tipper in the whole entire world. He's never so much as given me a dime for all the times he comes in here. Hardly says two words to you either. Ever since he won the lottery he has become even quieter than you could ever imagine. If it weren't for the gas station, the grocery store, and this here coffee shop, I don't think you'd see hide nor hair of him.

What is it about some people? If I won the lottery I would share it with everyone. I'd buy a new house for me and the kids. I'd pay off my car. I'd even give some to my ex. Not that he deserves any. But he did give me two fantastic kids. I don't hate him. I never said I hated him. I did say I wished he were dead, but that's not hating him. It's not the same thing.

If I won the lottery, I'd share it with my mom and brother and I'd buy some new bikes for the kids. I pay off my credit card debts. I know that I'd make it last. I'd probably still work here at the coffee shop. Maybe I'd even buy the coffee shop. I wouldn't change either. Now that I think of it, I'm starting to sound a lot like Mr. Owens. He didn't change much of anything in his life. No that's for sure. He was stingy before he won and he's just as stingy now.

"Watch what you wish for." Mr. Owens says to me quietly. "You think you want something, but the Good Lord only gives us what we are ready for."

Good Lord what is that old rich fart on about now?

"More coffee Mr. Owens?"

Mr. Owens points at my name tag, "Yours is Martha and mine is Bill."

"More coffee, Bill?"

"No thanks." Bill says as he pulls out a pocket watch.

"Is that a new pocket watch, Bill?" I ask.

"Time plays funny games with us."

"Pardon me?"

"If you get something before you can handle it, life goes to pieces."

"What exactly are you talking about Bill?"

"Just the ramblings of an old man."

Boy oh boy! Never heard Bill talk before. Be better if he just kept quiet.

"Could you get to the point."

"Let's say you got all the money you think your little heart desires."

"That'd be alright with me."

"I thought that too. Don't get me wrong. Money sure changed my life. When it came down to it, money was just about the last thing I wanted. I had it first on my list, but it was not what the doctor ordered."

"Are you alright Bill?"

"Martha. I wish for you what you wish for yourself. I just wanted to share with you that I wished for the same thing, once upon a time."

Well la dee da. I think his medication must be off.

Joe calls from the kitchen. "Martha, order for table twelve."

I mosey over and grab a plate of eggs and ham for table twelve.

Now there is a pretty sight, John Stevens. All six foot two, two hundred pounds. There's one hunk of a man. John Stevens is the likes as I've never seen in my bed. I'd sure get me the likes of John Stevens with a big purse full of money. Look at those eyes. Dreamboat! He's always kind and considerate too.

"Morning Martha." John says with a smile. "What was old man Owens on about?"

I bend down close so only John can hear, "I never seen him talk so much in my life." I look over to Mr. Owens' table, but he's gone. "My guess is the old man gives me two wooden nickels today. What a mood he was in."

I leave John and go over to pick up the dishes from Mr. Owens' table.

Well I'll be! A real quarter on a piece of paper.

I open the folded sheet of paper. A lottery ticket falls on the table. The sheet has a note hand written on it. The note reads:

Keep this quarter in a special place. One day you are going to need it, but that's a while away yet. Don't ask me how I know. Just trust me. More important, Trust Life. No matter what appears to be in your life, it always works out in your favour.
Your Guardian Angel Bill

My Guardian Angel Bill. What in the hell got into Mr. Owens today?

I slip the lottery ticket into my pocket.

I didn't even look at the ticket to be honest.

John calls over from his table, "What cha got there?"

"Nothing." I say holding the paper in my hand. "That's not true. Mr. Owens left me a real quarter tip and a note. Saying that I'll know when to use it."

"Aren't you the lucky one?"

"I guess so."

I picked up the kids after school.

"Hello beautiful." I say to Sarah as she runs up to me with her school bag dragging on the ground beside her.

"Money! Money! Money!" Sarah screams.

"What did you say?"

"Mommy! Mommy! Mommy!" Sarah screams again.

"Sarah, tell the truth. You did not say that."

"What?" She asks bewildered.

Aaron stands beside her. "That's what she said mom."

"Aaron. What are you saying? That I didn't hear Sarah correctly?"

"Are you alright mom?"

"Yeah. I'm fine. Let's go home."

At home the answering machine's red light flashes.

I have a sense of uneasiness as I press play. It's going to be some bill collector again. I've already got three calls this month. I missed one payment and now they are hounding me to pay up on everything.

"Hello Martha Evans, this is Visa Card Services calling you. We had a few questions about your account. If you could call us and talk directly to me, Sheila at extension 10576 at your earliest convenience it would be very appreciated."

Great. That sounds promising.

BEEP!

"Hello Martha. I can't get the kids this weekend. Something came up. Thanks. Bye."

Wow!

BEEP!

"Hello Martha. This is your guardian angel Bill calling. I trust you got my note. Have fun!"

What in God's green acre is he calling me at home for?

I pull out the lottery ticket again and look closely at it.

Funny, I never noticed that before. The date is circled on the ticket. This ticket is from . . . from January. No! It can't be! Oh my God! What if it is? Holy Moses! I can't believe it. I can't believe it. Calm down Martha! Calm! Calm! Oh my God! OH MY GOD!

Part 2

Where did Mr. Owens go? That is the question of a life time. Five months ago he changes my life forever. He leaves a lottery ticket as a tip. It's a lottery ticket he never cashed. Luckily it was still valid. If it had been only two months later, it would have been forfeited. They do that. They give you one year to cash your ticket.

I couldn't decide what to do. For a couple of weeks, I searched for Mr. Owens. I looked everywhere. I asked everyone. I even went over to Sherif Belford's office and asked them to help. They couldn't find him. He might as well have up and disappeared like a fart in the wind. Sherif Belford said that Mr. Owens' house on the point looked like no one had been living there in years.

Everyone remembers Mr. Owens. No one really knew him. He moved here a few years back. That's what people seem to recall. No one's even sure about that. He never talked and no one ever talked to him. The only reason anyone ever got wind of him is when Mrs. Windermere over at the hairdressers said she heard he won the lotto. Mrs. Windermere may very well be the town gossip, but she's usually got her story straight.

Nobody ever saw Mr. Owens spend too much. I guess he couldn't on a count of he never cashed the lottery ticket. There I was with a decision to make. I had a lottery ticket. Did I mention it was the winning lottery ticket? I had a winning lottery ticket, a quarter, and a note about the value of a quarter and trusting life.

I kept the quarter all right. I got it right here in my new wallet. One of those fancy Italian jobs with matching purse. It cost me three hundred dollars for the set. I said the money wouldn't change me, but it did. I got the heck out of that little town. I took the kids to the big city. Too many people in a small town know who *you are when you got money. I think most everyone who had ever been in that coffee shop, even once, wanted their share.*

The first one who wanted a share was my ex. How in tarnation did he hear about it. Not ten minutes after I finally cashed the ticket in the big city did I hear from him. It was uncanny how he knew. It was like a little bird told him or something.

"What cha up to, Martha?" Fred says to me as I walk out of the lottery building.

"Nothing."

"Come on now. We both know what you're doing here."

"I don't know what you mean."

"I hear different."

"What the hell are you talking about Fred?"

"Someone told me straight out that you'd won big and thought I should know about it."

Fred's got some big fancy lawyer from the city. He asking for half of it all on account of him taking care of the kids as much as he does. Now, that son of a gun is seeing the kids half the week and he says he'll take me to court if I don't do what's right.

"Kids need their father." he says to me with his lawyer standing beside him.

I wanted to settle out of court. I'd give him a million if he let me be. That's not going to happen. He can be a mean son of a bitch. I mean a mean son of a gun. Where does he get off thinking he deserves half of this money? It was given to me as a gift and all. I can't let him rule my life anymore. My lawyer says that I only have to prove that Fred never showed up when he said he was going to and I'll do fine.

The proving part has been a little hard. Then two day ago, in the mail, some pictures arrived. The kind of pictures you don't want your mother to see. I admit that I had some fun with my new found money. I went down to Mexico. All I can say is those were two of the nicest people I've ever met. A couple from California they were. Now that the pictures came to the house I have to wonder how much fun is too much? I know for sure that Fred got those pictures. It was a typed letter, unsigned, but it's got to be him.

Of all the low down dirty things I've ever seen, that takes the cake. What is it about money that brings out the worst in some people? I've kept this away from the kids as best I can. Then just a few days ago, someone at school mentioned that they knew the kids were rich because of our new car. It's just a Jaguar. That doesn't make someone rich.

I haven't been working. I always wanted to paint. So I got all the stuff to paint. I got a studio in the house. I bought the nicest house you ever did see. It has five bedrooms. It's in a beautiful neighbourhood. It's a gated community with it's own police force. The kids are safe here. It's way better than where we used to live. Small town life is for small time people. I love the pool. Love it. Indoor pool, I can swim every day of my life until I die. Which wont be for a very long time, considering how much money I have.

I never said how much it was, did I? The lottery ticket was for seven million, two hundred and seventy six thousand, four hundred and twelve dollars. That's a lot of bazollies. I divided one million up amongst my family; my parents, my brother, my aunts and uncles, my grandparents, my cousins. I gave some of it to my *friends. I gave ten percent to charity. I gave it to the hospital in my old town. I had been in that hospital a few times and they needed the help. They named a new ward after me. I didn't want that, but what's done is done.*

I guess what's really bothering me is that after all the money I shared and the stuff I bought, well I don't really have half to give to Fred. My lawyer says I'd have to sell the house in order to do it. I was lucky I got a financial advisor at least. The same day Fred surprised me at the lotto building, there was a phone message at home.

BEEP!

"Mrs. Evans, my name is Peter Mitchell. I am a financial advisor down at the bank. Congratulations! I heard from Judy at the coffee shop that you came into some money. I just wanted to say that a win-fall of this nature can change a person's life. I hope that you'll come down and meet with me. I want you to be aware of some of your options. When you bring your Lotto Cheque into the bank, I would like to share with you some investment options in very simple no-nonsense terms."

BEEP!

I called and met Mr. Peter Mitchell. He's an Investment Broker. He had a few other people with him too. There was Cynthia Donaldson. She was a real estate broker. She got us our house in the big city here. There was Tanya Koops. She does small business loans and business plans. They were all real nice down to earth people. Salt of the earth as my dad says.

They invited me into a boardroom at the bank. They had coffee and muffins laid out. They had even bought them from my coffee shop. The one I used to work at, that is. They also had tea and juice. I had a big cup of coffee. Then they got down to business.

Peter Mitchell starts, "Martha, now that you've met everyone here, we want to get a sense of how you are feeling about your new found wealth?"

"It's pretty damn amazing!"

Both Cynthia and Tanya nod their heads and smile.

"Now that you've had this huge influx of cash, what would you like to accomplish with it?" Tanya asks.

"I've had a few days to think about this. I was originally thinking I'd like to buy the coffee shop."

"I could help you with that investment." Tanya says.

"Well that was what I was originally thinking."

"Yes of course." Tanya regroups, "What are you thinking now?"

"This morning as I prepared to get the cheque," I pull out the cheque for seven million, two hundred and seventy six thousand, four hundred and twelve dollars, and set it on the table in front of me and still hold onto it. "I was thinking, I didn't really want to be a big fish in a little pond. I thought I should move to the big city with the kids and start a new life where we would have room to grow."

Cynthia smiles, "A new home in a new city."

"Definitely need that. I got some people I want to share some of the money with. I want to give some to the hospital. I would like to get a new home and a new car. Aside from that I just want this new found wealth to provide for me and the kids for many years to come."

"That's a very good wish." Peter says, "We can help you make that wish a reality."

"Yes I'd like some help. I heard that most lottery winners go back to where they were or worse in five years time."

"I've heard that too." Peter says.

"I don't want that to happen. Do you have any suggestions?"

"A good financial team is something you're going to need."

"Doesn't that cost money?"

"I don't want you to be spending any money without feeling good and informed about it. Do you read much, Martha?"

"I read romance novels and thrillers."

"I've been know to enjoy them from time to time myself."

Cynthia and Tanya and I look at Peter awkwardly.

"I mean the thrillers that is."

We all laugh.

"My suggestion before you do anything is to read three short books before you make any decisions with the bulk of your money. Of course pay off your immediate bills and buy yourself a few nice things. We can set that all up for you at the bank. I'd personally be able to take care of your bills for you as well as set you up with a steady amount of money for the next couple of weeks until we can discuss what you've read. How does that sound?"

"It sounds a lot like school, Mr. Mitchell."

"This is a very different schooling than what you got in school. If you'll trust me on this one, I think these three books will change the way you look at money. Now, we'll deposit your money into a special account. This is the type of account you can only get when you have the kind of money you now have. You've reached a whole new level of money. There are things you'll be able to experience at this new level that you could never have participated in before. The one challenge with this new level is it comes with a whole bunch of different rules. Rules you may probably never even heard about. If you agree with this little proposal of reading three small books, I'll take care of your bills and place $10,000 into your present bank account to spend. What do you say to all this?"

"It kind of sounds like I'm not getting my money here."

"It's your money Martha. You yourself said that you didn't want to be one of those statistics that ends up in an even tougher spot than before."

"That's true enough."

So that afternoon I officially quit at the coffee shop. They figured I was gonna do that and I did. I went home and got all my bills together and I just dropped them off at the bank. Peter took care of them all. I didn't even have to think about them. Then I picked up the kids after school. I wanted to go out for dinner to

celebrate. The kids chose the McDonald's by the Highway 17 bypass. It wasn't exactly where I wanted to dine, but it made the kids happy.

Then I went home and stared at the three books that Peter gave me to read. Actually Peter only gave me one book. It was called The Generosity Factor. *Cynthia gave me* Mr. Everit's Secret. *And Tanya gave me* Rich Dad Poor Dad.

I had heard of Rich Dad Poor Dad, *so I read it first. All the books gave me chills of recognition when I read them. It was like a whole different world of money thoughts opened up within me. They all talked about my thoughts being the basis for my financial position all these years. I don't fully know about all that, but I do know that I had never thought about using money in the ways these books said. When I had finished reading all the books I set up another appointment at the bank.*

Everyone is present for this meeting.

"So what did you think of the books?" Peter asks.

"Each of them had different things. Some of the same things too. I read them in three days, as you know, and they gave me way too much to think about and a whole bunch of questions to ask."

"Go ahead." Tanya says.

"First, here are the main points I got from each of the books. *Rich Dad Poor Dad* reminded me to buy assets instead of liabilities. *Mr. Everit's Secret* reminded me that no pain means no pain and that life doesn't have to be a struggle. And *The Generosity Factor* reminded me to create a life of Significance.

"I never much speak of God in the way that these books do, but I think about God is a similar way. I see God as this energy all around us. I only have to feel connected with it to experience it all. I admit that I have not always felt connected with all of life. Especially with my ex."

Everyone chuckles.

"So I guess these are my questions. I still want to give ten percent to the local hospital here. I want to share one million dollars with my family and friends. How can I get the best value for the rest of my money?"

"That's only one question." Cynthia notes.

"I suspect you all are going to share a whole bunch of answers with me."

They laugh.

"Money is less about the amount you have and more about what you believe about money." Peter says.

"I can see that now."

"Cynthia and Tanya and I belong to a group of young investors in town. We are a few years older than you are, but we are young in the investment circles. I'm sure you've heard the term *Old Money*?"

"Sure."

"*Old Money* for us is not about people who have inherited it, it's about people who are comfortable with it. Lotto winners are part of *New Money*. That's why so many lotto winners seem to end up without their money in a relatively short period of time. *Old Money* people have solid beliefs about money and they attract money with everything they do. Most particularly the way they think about money. *New Money* can learn all the same things. That's what we hope to share with you Martha. *New Money* becomes *Old Money* when you are conscious about your money choices.

"So I am *New Money* who would benefit a whole bunch by thinking like *Old Money*."

Tanya smiles, "Definitely."

That was six months ago. Today I have some problems around money with my ex. We go to court at ten this morning. My lawyer says it's all gonna work out. "No problemo!" were his exact words.

I have set up my money to make me more money. I invested in a small apartment building. I only had to make a down payment. The monthly rents take care of the mortgage and gives me a few dollars extra. Once the mortgage is paid off I'm going to be set for life with monthly cash flow. It's not a big apartment. It has twenty-two units. Even if I lost everything, but had the apartment, I'd make enough positive cash flow to live without ever having to work again. If I keep my budget real.

I am so grateful to everyone in my life. First Bill, my guardian angel. I don't know who he was or why he gave me that lottery ticket, but he changed my life forever.

I love my kids. Aaron and Sarah have been really good about everything. They're young enough that they haven't even been bothering me. I got us a new house with their own bedrooms and it's great. I filled their rooms with new furniture and got them new bikes and skateboards. I got them a pool. Sure I got it for me too.

RING!

Who calling this early in the morning?

RING!

I pick up the phone.

"Hello."

"Hello, Martha."

"Hi mom."

"How's things?"

What's she up to?

"Fine mom. Is everything okay?"

"Sure. I'm fine."

Who isn't then?

"It's Jimmy." Mom bursts into tears. "He left."

"What?"

"He took the money and ran."

She's crying hard. I never much liked Jimmy. I'm just glad I didn't have to live with him. Jimmy was my mom's second husband. My dad and mom divorced after I finished high school.

"Are you serious?"

"Yes!"

27

"Mom, I'm sorry."

"I need money."

"Pardon?"

"I need money. My pension is not enough to live on."

Not now. Dear God in heaven, I got enough on my plate.

"Are you there Martha?"

"Yes."

"Can you send me some money today?"

"Mom right now is not a good time . . . "

More tears.

"I don't have . . . "

Sobbing. Heavy breathing. Calm down mom. It'll be okay.

"Mom, I have to go."

"You can send me the money today by *Western Union* and the money would get there instantly."

New Money beliefs. Wow!

"Mom, I can't send you the money."

"What?" Mom says shocked, "After all the hours of labour it took me to get you out. You're so selfish."

"Mom, thank you for sharing your opinion. I got to go."

"Wait. This is important."

"Bye mom."

I hang up.

Wow! I can't help my mom. I got all of my money into investments: the apartment, some stocks and bonds, this house. I don't have a bank account full of cash as she seems to imagine. Sure I have enough to meet and exceed my current needs each month, but that's it.

RING!

Now who is that?

"Hello?"

"Good morning Martha." *It's my lawyer Ken.* "We got a big day ahead of us. How are you this morning?"

"Good. My mom called asking for money a few minutes ago. Her current husband just left her and took the cash."

"That's sounds bad, and I don't mean to seem heartless, but we have to focus on the job at hand today. Can you put this stuff about your mom out of your mind?"

"Yeah."

"Good we are going to need to be of one mind today. I just got a folder dropped at my door this morning. Seems we are going to have some trouble at the courthouse."

"What do you mean?"

"I'll pick you up in ten minutes. I'm on my way to your

house right now. Are you ready to go?"

"I'll meet you outside."

I settle into Ken's BMW.

"Good morning."

"Here's the folder I found outside my door this morning."

I bet it's the Mexico pictures.

I open the folder. It's a court document. Fred's name and my name are on it.

"What's this Ken?"

"It's divorce papers."

Oh shit!

"Why didn't you tell me you weren't divorced?"

"You never asked."

"You always said, he was your ex."

"What are you saying?"

"They've offered to settle this out of court with the divorce papers signed. Fred wants half. He'll probably get it."

"That's not fair."

"No it's not. His lawyer kept this from us to force

something even worse."

"What?"

"Look at the next page."

I turn the page and there is another court document. Fred's name is on it again, "What's this one Ken?"

"They'll apply for custody to get all the money."

"I've been taking care of those kids ever since he left us high and dry for some tart at his work."

"That's why they sent us the next page."

I flip to the page. *There's the Mexico pictures. Thank God most of the picture has black tape across the appropriate parts. My face is uncovered, so you can clearly see it is me. The woman's breast I'm kissing is mostly covered though.*

"They won't be able to use this picture in court, but they'll be able to put it forward. Even if it gets stricken from the record. They'll probably win."

"What do you mean they'll probably win? I thought this was open and shut. You said this was easy!"

"They have changed the playing field a whole heck of a lot."

That son of a bitch! How can he do this to me? What did I ever do to him?

"What do you suggest?"

"You have to make a decision. Either way it's not too

pretty. If we settle out of court, their gonna ask for your assets to be liquidated. If we go to court, they might get it all."

"Wow."

"I think you have to figure out what is more important to you."

"I want my kids. That's the most important thing."

"Well that was an easy decision."

"Yeah."

In the court house, Fred stands waiting with his lawyer.

"You sure fixed this."

"You fixed it Martha. I just put your broken pieces together."

"You set me up."

"That's rich. I didn't go to Mexico for some holiday delight."

"No, you went to your office."

Ken grabs my arm as if to say hold back.

"My client is ready to sign the divorce papers." Ken says.

"My client has decided to go ahead with the case. Fred wants what's best for the kids."

"You coward." I say. "You can have it all, including the kids. Where do I sign?"

Ken looks at me, "Martha are you sure?"

I nod my head.

"I need to speak with my client for a moment."

Ken pulls me over beside a pillar on the other side of the hall.

"What are you doing? A few minutes ago you were saying you wanted the kids."

"I'm calling his bluff."

"You're giving him what he wants."

"He doesn't want the kids. He wants the money."

"What if you're wrong?"

"We'll find out real fast."

"If you sign away on your kids there is no way you can get them back, unless Fred signs them back to you. You don't want to do this."

"This appears to be the only choice I have."

"We always have more choices. I can get the court date delayed due to this new information. It will buy us some time."

"I don't need time. I need my life back."

I fiddle with my Italian purse.

"Is everything okay?"

"No everything is not okay. I just need a few damn minutes to think."

"Don't be rash. I'll get the postponement. We'll regroup."

"Why bother? Fred's new money hungry."

"What?"

"Nothing. I say give it all to him. Will you still get a fee, Ken?"

"Yes."

"Good let's do it then."

"Are you all right?"

"I'm fine. Fred was the one who drunk us dry. He'll get his comeuppance."

"Martha are you sure?"

"I've never been more sure in my life."

Ken and I walk back over to Fred and his Lawyer.

Ken speaks, "My client is prepared to sign it all over to Mr. Sparks."

"That's agreeable. However Mr. Sparks is prepared to let Mrs. Evans keep the children."

"How giving of you Fred."

"I'm also going to give you an apartment in your ... I mean in my apartment building at a reduced rate for the kids sake."

"You're all heart. Where do I sign?"

Fred's Lawyer had the papers ready. The papers never even included the child custody papers. It was about getting it all. I am happy to oblige. I trust he'll get everything that's coming to him. I know I'll get everything that's coming to me.

I was left with the three thousand dollars I had in the bank. Ken took care of all the paper work. He signed everything over to Fred. We moved out of our house by month's end. Aaron and Sarah were disappointed.

"Why mom?" Aaron asks. "I like this school."

"You're still going to the same school."

"I liked the house too. Can't we just live with dad?"

"Your father and I are no longer compatible. We just have different ideas about the way to live. Both your dad and I are trying the best we can to live the best life we know how."

"Mom?"

"Yes, Sarah?"

"Couldn't you go to counselling?"

"No. I know you both miss your dad. He's a great father to you kids, but we're definitely finished. As I told you before it was nothing either of you did. We just found out we had separate interests."

"What about the pool mom?"

"We have a pool in the new building we're moving into."

"Really?" Aaron says.

"Yeah. It's shared with other people. I'm sure there'll even be some kids there."

"Cool." Sarah says.

That next month was the hardest. The kids put on the best face they could, but they were upset. I did not take Fred's reduced rate offer. The motel we moved into was not what the kids expected. It had a pool, but there were no kids. One weekend there was, but they were teenagers and not really willing to play nice.

I was depressed. Fred let me keep the Jaguar, but it was too much of a car for our life. I traded it in for a used Volkswagen camper and some cash. School was going to be over for the kids in two more weeks. Then we were going to pack up and go travelling cross country. My heart wasn't into it, but it gave me something to look forward to.

I called my mom a couple of days ago to tell her what had happened at the courthouse.

"Hello."

"Mom, it's Martha."

"Well, thanks for sending the money."

"The money's gone mom."

"What do you mean the money's gone?"

"Fred has it all."

"How could you do a stupid thing like that?"

"Sometimes these things happen."

"First you married that loser Fred and now you lost all your money. Don't say I never told you so."

"Good bye mom."

The kids were at school and I took a hot shower. The scalding water caressed my body and soothed my aching muscles. That's when I started to cry. I was sputtering and struggling to breathe through the tears. For all the Bravado I had had at the courthouse, now I was just a little girl with no friends to play with and hardly any toys either. I had a Volkswagen camper van and just enough money in the bank for food and rent for a couple months, and gas for the camper. That's all that was left. In the shower I broke down and cried and prayed.

I don't think that life is supposed to be like this. Really, is it supposed to be a struggle? Am I supposed to never have enough? Why do so many people around me seem to have more than I have? When will I ever have enough? What do I have to do God? Just tell me! Please I beg you to tell me! What have I done to deserve this? Am I not right in some way? I've done mostly good things. I've done some bad. Overall I am a good person. I really am a good person. Please help me!

Part 3

W*e're singing. I love singing. We're driving down the highway. We're driving around the mountain and singing 'She's Coming Round The Mountain'. We've been going on for what seems like half an hour and we're making up our own verses.*

"She'll be riding six white horses when she comes."

"She'll be sitting on the horse with six guns."

"She'll be sitting at the table with six nuns."

"She'll be sitting on the toilet with the runs."

"Mom!" Sarah says.

"Yes?"

"Can we sing something else."

"We'll be singing something different when we're done." I sing.

"We'll be singing something different because it's fun." Aaron sings.

"Please!"

"You always spoil it." Aaron says.

"Aaron please? Sarah's asked us to stop and I have to admit that this song is getting way past where this song should ever

41

be sung."

"Fine."

"Why don't you read that magazine I bought you."

Aaron sings, *"I'll be reading that magazine as you drive. "*

"MOM!"

"Aaron, take a time out."

"What did I do?"

"Would you like you're time doubled?"

Aaron stays quiet.

"Mom?"

"Yes, Sarah?"

"Where are we going exactly?"

"I thought we'd drive to the ocean."

"The real ocean."

"Of course the real ocean." Aaron says from the back seat.

"Aaron your time is now doubled."

"Whatever."

"Mom are we going to go back to that motel after the summer?"

"No."

"Where are we going to live?"

"What do you think about staying by the ocean?"

"What about all my friends." Aaron asks.

"We can talk about this after your time out."

"That's not fair."

"You'll make new friends."

"When were you going to tell us?"

"I just did."

"This is wrong!"

"Wrong?"

"Yes wrong! There has to be laws against this sort of thing."

"Aaron calm down."

"AAAARRRRGGGGHHHHH!"

Aaron kicks the back of the seat.

I pull the camper over to the side of the road for safety and look Aaron in the eyes.

"Are you trying to kill us?"

"You're the one who's taking my life away!"

"You're being melodramatic."

"Mom." Aaron pauses, "Screw you!"

"Aaron . . ."

"- - You tie our bikes onto this stupid van. Make us pack our stuff up and now I understand why. That's the cheapest thing you have ever done. I can't believe this. First you leave dad and now you leave my life behind in two different towns in less than a year. I hate you! I hate you! I hate you!"

Aaron opens the door to the camper and gets out with his knapsack and walks down the highway with a thumb out hitchhiking.

"Aaron you get back in here this instant."

"You can't make me."

"Aaron Presley Sparks, you get in here *now*."

"That's another thing. Presley! Why Presley?"

Aaron walks away. A car drives by. I get out and walk towards him. "It's just a name."

"Stay away from me."

"Aaron please?"

"Whatever gave you the idea that you could just take us away from everything again?"

"I'm trying to protect you and your sister."

"The only thing we need protection from is you."

"I'm sorry okay. I should have told you, but I hadn't even decided any of this until just now. I thought living at the ocean would be a good idea when I said it and now I can see that it wasn't."

"You better believe it wasn't. I don't believe you. We packed everything up. We left that hotel behind. You knew before now."

"I swear I didn't. I thought that we might find some cool place where our life would totally change for the better, but that's it."

Sarah calls from the camper, "Stop fighting."

"We're not fighting. We're talking."

"It sounds like fighting."

"We're not fighting."

"Please stop."

"We're almost done. Just turn on some music okay."

"Okay." Sarah says.

I turn back to Aaron who is waving down a car vigorously. The car pulls over to the side of the road and the driver speaks out the window. "Everything alright?"

"Yes." I say.

"No!" Aaron says.

"We're just having a disagreement."

"I thought something was wrong."

"We'll be fine once we work this out." I say.

"No we wont. Take me with you." Aaron counters.

"Sorry son. I'm going to side with your mom on this one."

"She's not my mom."

"Aaron stop that."

"I've never seen her before in my life. She drugged me. I woke up in her van in the middle of nowhere. To get away I said I had to go to the bathroom."

I grab Aaron by the arm. "Aaron Presley Sparks, that's enough out of you." I turn to the driver, "Thanks for your concern. We'll be alright once we get over this disagreement."

"Alright. You okay son?"

"Sure, just leave me with this crazed woman. When you read about it in the papers don't feel guilty."

I grab Aaron by the ear, "That's enough Aaron."

"I'm sorry mom! I'm sorry!"

"Are you sure you guys are going to be okay?" The driver asks again.

"It's nothing we wont get past after a time out."

"I'm not taking a time out!"

"Not you Aaron. Me."

"Well you have a safe trip now."

"Thank you." I smile and wave as the driver pulls away from us.

"Don't you ever do that again."

"You first!"

"Fine. I wont take you away from a place without telling you what's what. Agreed?"

"Agreed."

We walk back to the camper. We all take a bathroom break and a time out before we get back in. I turn the key and the sound of an engine unable to turn over fills the air. I turn the key to off and try again. Nothing.

"Shit!"

"Mom!"

"Sorry Sarah."

I try again. Nothing. I hit my hands on the steering wheel.

"What did I do to deserve this?"

I jump out of the camper, slam the door shut, and kick the front tire so hard that it feels like I broke a toe.

"Damn it! Why me? What did I do? What!"

Sarah sticks her head out the window.

"Mom is everything okay?"

I don't say a word.

"Mom will be fine." Aaron says to Sarah, "I think she got her period today."

"I did not! Where would you ever get an idea like that? Never mind. I should never have let you guys stay with your father."

●●●

Not a single car in either direction for over an hour now. I can't take this anymore. I saw an emergency phone box back a ways and I just hope it's not too far for Sarah. Wait a minute we have the bikes.

"Aaron, untie the bikes."

"Mom?"

"You heard me. Untie the bikes so we can get to that emergency phone a ways back."

"Mom some car is going to come."

"The sun is going to go down in a couple of hours and I want to be somewhere other than on this highway at night. So untie those bikes please."

"I could ride to the phone myself."

"That's not a good idea. We'll go together. When we can see the phone, then you can ride ahead, but not before then."

I help Aaron untie the bikes and we start on our way.

I didn't see another car the entire time it took us to go to the emergency phone. By the time we got near, Aaron had forgot all about wanting to ride ahead to the phone. We were talking about being at the ocean and living at our own house there. I didn't know how to tell the kids that dream may not happen so we just dreamed about it together and it felt good.

At the phone, I pick up the receiver and wait for someone to answer. It rings seven times and I am getting a bit nervous until someone picks up the other end.

"Hello Martha." Bill says.

"Bill?"

"Your one and only guardian angel."

"I need help."

"Everything seems to be right on schedule."

"On schedule?"

"Your journey to trusting life."

"Can you send some help?"

"I can't do that."

"What?"

"God does that. Help is on the way. Just not in the way you would ever imagine."

"Bill is this some joke?"

"Like a cosmic joke. That's funny Martha. No everything in life always works out in your favour, no matter what appears to be."

"You said that in the note. What does that note mean?"

"Trust life! It can't be more simple than that?"

"Sure it can. Can you give me a hint?"

"Okay. I think it was Einstein who said, 'There are two ways we can look at life. We can see everything as a miracle or nothing as a miracle.' Does that help?"

"You're saying that my broken down camper is a miracle."

"Einstein was saying there are two ways you can look at it."

"What about that quarter?"

"You'll understand when the time is right. You'll probably want to head back to your camper now."

"We're tired can't our help pick us up here?"

"No one is getting this call, Martha"

"What do you mean?"

"Ask Sarah. Until we speak again, bye Martha. Remember, trust life."

The line goes dead. There is no dial tone. It is silent. I look over at Sarah. She is spinning in a circle, a yellow ribbon follows her path and a piece of paper is attached to the very end of it dragging in the sand.

"What do you have there Sarah?" I ask as I walk towards

her.

"Just a ribbon mom."

"Where did you get it?"

Sarah stops spinning. "It was attached to the phone booth."

"The phone booth? May I see that?"

I reach forward and grab the yellow ribbon from Sarah. Red letters, clearly apparent now say, 'do not cross'. On the letter size paper is a photocopied sign in a plastic slip cover that says, 'OUT OF ORDER, next emergency phone booth five miles in either direction. Sorry for any inconvenience.' My face must look quite the sight.

Aaron asks, "Is everything okay mom?"

"The man on the phone said it was going to be okay. We better head back to the camper."

Where is the camper? It couldn't have been much farther than this? All these low hills look the same. I didn't think it was this far.

The sun is low on the horizon now.

We're all tired. Sarah is very tired. I have a bad feeling about all of this. The tire tracks in the sand confirm it. The camper is gone.

"NO!" I cry out.

"What mom?"

I open my purse and rifle through it. The keys are not there.

"I'm so stupid. I am dumber than dumb. I am an idiot. Idiot! Idiot! Idiot!"

Aaron moves forward and hugs me and whispers in my ear, "You're scaring Sarah."

I stop immediately. "Sarah come give us a hug."

Sarah joins us.

"The man on the phone said that someone was on the way."

"What about our camper?"

"The man said that it was going to happen in some way that we never expected."

"You mean someone took our camper ahead to the garage?"

"Maybe. That thought feels a lot better, doesn't it?"

Sarah smiles and then she gets a sad look on her face, "What about Pokey?"

Pokey her favourite teddy bear.

"Pokey too. Either that or he escaped and found his family again with his bear wife and their cubs."

Sarah hugs me tighter.

The sun drops below the horizon. It's going to get cold very soon. Just then the head lights of a car come in the direction we are heading. I take a deep breath and wait until the car pulls up beside us.

"Hi there?" A kind looking older man says. "Where are you folks headed?"

Sarah brightens up, "The ocean."

"Well just happens that I'm headed that way. I see you have you transportation taken care of, but could I give you a lift?"

"That'd be real nice sir."

"I was just about to stop at the diner up the road, would you care to join me for some food?"

Aaron speaks first "Yes!"

"It's settled then. Let's get your bikes in the trunk."

With the bikes in the trunk, we drive not more than a mile up the road to a gas station and diner.

If we'd gone the other way, we'd have been to the diner and back to the camper in no time. I can't believe how dumb a mistake I made.

"My name is Martha. This is my daughter, Sarah. And my son, Aaron."

"Pleased to meet you all. My name is Charles Smith."

"Mr. Smith. You saved us a whole heap of a lot."

"Call me Charles. All my friends do."

"Thanks Charles."

At the diner I share the story of our day with Charles .

"If we'd have gone just over this hill in the other direction we would have been there and back and on our way earlier today with our camper."

"True enough. But you never would have met me." Charles smiles.

"It's been our pleasure." I say.

The kids say thanks and then get right back to hungrily eating their meals.

"The kids just love their cheese burgers and fries."

"They're going to grow up big and strong like their mother."

"Some days I'm not so strong."

"Sure you are. Could you imagine if what had happened would have happened to someone who was weaker?"

"You didn't see me earlier today. You didn't see me a couple of months ago."

"I didn't see you when you were a kid growing up either. I only see you right now."

"Right now, I'm a mess inside, Mr. Smith."

"Charles, please call me Charles."

"Charles."

"Do I really look that old?"

"I was just taught to treat my elders with respect."

"It's official, I am as old as your parents, am I?"

"I don't know about that."

"I tell you I'm older."

"You're not that old."

"In the scheme of things I still feel like a kid at heart."

"I sure wish I did."

"For me it's all about attitude. It was Einstein who said 'There is only one question that all of science and philosophy seek to answer: is the universe a friendly place?' It sure is one heck of a lot friendlier from a child's perspective."

"That's weird you should mention Einstein. Someone earlier today mentioned Einstein."

"Who knows maybe that means you're on the right track."

"Maybe."

After dinner I reach for my purse to pay. Mr. Smith holds out his hand and waves me away, "It's my treat."

"What do you say kids?"

"Thanks Mr. Smith."

"Please call me Charles."

After dinner, Charles offered to take us to the police station in the next town. I made a decision in that moment to let go of whatever I imagined was supposed to happen. At the station, I filed a report and said to myself all the while, 'trust life'.

Charles then said we could stay at his house until we got settled near the beach. It was late when we finally arrived. I could smell the salty sea air so I knew we were close, but we were all so tired after an exhausting day, we crashed just as soon as we got there. I woke up in the morning to the smell of fresh coffee and the kids screaming and playing.

"Mom! Mom! Get up!" Sarah shakes me gently.

"It's the ocean mom!" Aaron says. "Charles took us down while you slept, but you've got to get up and see it."

I brush the sleep from my eyes. I wander out with a slow sway because I am half asleep. On the table is a cup of fresh coffee.

"Good morning Martha." Charles says.

"Morning."

"Mom can we go and play outside?" Aaron asks.

"Yeah."

I am stunned by the view. Not in a million years would I have got us into a place with such a stunning view as this. Windows from floor to ceiling. The ceiling is two stories high. The balcony is accented by shoots of grass and then sand down to the beach and ocean as far as the horizon.

"Is this heaven Charles?"

"I guess you could say that. I think of heaven as that place where love is all you see. From my vantage point all I see is love here. I took the kids for a walk down the beach earlier. They were way too excited this morning. I didn't want them waking you."

"Thanks. I needed the rest."

"I was thinking. If it doesn't put you out too much, I'd like you to stay with me for a while."

"Put us out. I think you mean put you out."

"It's been quite a few years now since I've had company."

"What about your family?"

"My wife Shirley moved on years ago, to a different stage of life."

"I'm sorry to hear that."

"Why? It was her time."

"Kids?"

"We never had any. We were too busy with other things."

"That must be nice, All I seem to be is too busy with kids."

"There can be a happy balance."

"I look forward to that day."

"Today is that day Martha. Right now all of your dreams are coming true."

"Maybe from your vantage point Charles, but from mine it doesn't look like all of my dreams are coming true."

57

"Well if they're not your dreams, Martha, whose dreams are you living?"

"Losing my money is my dream? Losing my camper is my dream?"

"It looks to me like you're showered with blessings from my vantage point."

"You don't know where I've been."

"I only know where you are. Where you are is the only place you are ever going to be. This moment is all you ever have."

"Great."

"Seriously. You have more than enough of whatever it is you think you need right now."

"I don't see that."

"You're right. you don't. Lot of good it's going to be with me telling you what you have, because if you don't see it, it just doesn't matter. It might as well not even exist. I can see all your blessings, but they can't bless you unless you bless yourself with them."

"Humor me Charles. Show me where I have more than enough in my life right now?"

"You have more than enough life force keeping you alive. You have more than enough love from those kids. You have more than enough abundance of a hot coffee and a beautiful view. You have more than enough peace, health, joy, and success. I'm not talking about what you'd like to accomplish or what you think is missing. I'm talking about what is available right here right now."

"I can sort of see that."

"All you have to see is the possibilities."

"I guess."

"That's what life is all about. See what's possible over what appears to be and you'll live you're dreams."

"What are you talking about Charles?"

"All of life is made up of illusions. We call these illusions reality, but they are only one possible reality."

"There are more realities."

"As many as there are people."

"You mean that everyone sees reality differently?"

"Have you ever heard of the definition of a genius?"

"I guess so."

"Here's my definition. A genius makes illusions real. A genius is a person who sees something no one else can see, and then reveals it for everyone else to see."

"Are you a genius?"

"I reveal things just like you. We all create our experience by imagining what is possible until it becomes actual."

"Is anything possible?"

"I think so. More important is what do you think?"

"I'm not sure."

"The more you are sure about what you think, the more you experience what you think. It's when you keep changing what you think about that you keep changing what you experience."

"Maybe after I have my coffee and some food this will make sense."

"Blessings on your food."

I love the beach. Charles has an amazing place. I would love to live in a place like this. I don't want to overstay my welcome. Charles is like the perfect grandfather and the Dalai Lama all wrapped into one. I read an article on the Dalai Lama once that said he's full of laughter. That's Charles exactly. He's always laughing with us. I love talking with him too. He knows so much about life. If I didn't know it, I would swear that Charles works in some cosmic guardian angel school. Who knows maybe he works with Bill.

"Charles?" I say at dinner one day. "Why do you think we met up?"

"It was Divine intervention."

"Really?"

"Yes. I had been driving on the interstate that day, when I got this hankering for the hamburgers from that diner we went to. I was sitting there in the car thinking it was going to take me three-quarters of an hour out of my way, but there it was. I wanted a burger from that diner. A picture of the diner flashed in my mind with a picture of a juicy burger, clear as day. I follow that kind of calling."

"That sounds more like you were hungry."

"There was a restaurant right at the first turn off. If I just wanted to eat, I could have stopped there."

"But Divine intervention?"

"Who am I to argue? I always follow those kind of hunches now and they've never let me down. A long time ago I didn't always follow those suggestions. I've made my share of mistakes. That's why I listen when I get the call. Have you ever got the call?"

"I don't know. Maybe. Probably. No floating burgers though."

"Maybe when you get older. I think wisdom is a combination of experience and listening to the suggestions. It gets easier for you as you get older when you trust that life works out the way it's supposed to."

"Trust . . . I hope so."

"It's just as easy now at your age too."

"How do you figure that?"

"It's all about feeling."

"Feeling?"

"If it feels good I'm usually on the right track."

"That's it?"

"That's it. It's when I feel bad that I know I'm going the wrong way. When it's frustrating and hard and a struggle, I usually stop myself and head in the exact opposite direction. Right towards ease and joy."

"I like that. Does that work for everything?"

"For me it does."

"What about for money problems?"

"Money's no problem. Ideas about money can be though. If you focus on money problems, you're going to experience more money problems. If you focus on money joy, you're going to experience money joy."

"Let's say I've got a big debt. What do I do?"

"You make a plan which includes your money joy and see how it feels."

"Could you explain that a little."

"Sure. Let's say you have five thousand dollars in credit card debt. You plan to stop using your credit cards and make monthly payments that are larger than the interest until you pay off all the money. You think about the plan and it feels good."

"So I follow the plan?"

"Sure, it'll work. It feels good because it's taking you in the direction of credit card freedom."

"What about if you continue to use your cards? Let's say you're out of a job and you have to use your credit cards to feed your family."

"It's the same thing. You make a plan, in this case to use your credit cards to pay for your food. Having the means to provide food for your family makes you feel good, so you know you are on the right track."

"I'm confused. Those are two very different actions."

"Actually they are two different intentions and different intentions create very different outcomes."

"Are you saying that for every person's intention there is a different outcome."

"I didn't say it, you just did. If you take that thought to it's ultimate conclusion, there are almost seven billion intentions creating on the planet right now. We all experience life the way we think about it. If you want to experience new things in your life, all you have to do is start thinking about new things."

"If you believe it, you can achieve it."

"That's it exactly. Plus whatever you are achieving in your life right now is what you are actually believing at some level."

"That kind of sucks."

"Only if you don't use it to your benefit."

"Benefit?"

"The more you use something the easier it becomes."

"Does this work for the good and the bad."

"It's only a direction. If that direction feels good to you, then God is guiding you to that experience. Don't kill the messenger."

"Are you saying that everyone in life is guided by God."

"I believe so."

"So violence is okay?"

"Life is okay. Violence is one way you can choose to experience life. I like to experience the goodness inside of everyone. A so-called bad person is only a person expressing the energy of life through them. It may appear to feel good to them, but more often than not they usually feel bad. No matter what, God lets us experience whatever we choose. We're all trying to experience the most fulfilling life as we choose to define it."

"Even murderers?"

"The extremes are not the norm. We are all constructed from the energy of the universe. Without these so-called bad people in your life, how could you experience your goodness?"

"You've lost me."

"Bad things happen to good people because they believe in them on some level and because they need something bad to let their goodness shine against. But you don't have to experience life that way, you can shine your good against good too."

"Charles, are you an angel?"

Charles laughs heartily, "You crack me up Martha. I went to the school of life."

●●●

A walk on the beach is so refreshing. Aaron and Sarah are playing barefoot in the waves. My mind, as usual, is full of thoughts. Millions of thoughts about life.

Charles has gone into town to run some errands. I know

that soon enough it'll be time for us to find our own place, although I love that we've had this break. I needed this break.

The beach has fewer people now that summer is nearing the end. I've been looking at the local schools. I want to stay here.

"Aaron, Sarah, come here please?"

"Just a minute mom."

They bunny hop over the waves in unison together. *Sarah is doing well considering how much younger she is.* I sit down on a rock on the shore. When they are done they come over and join me.

Aaron speaks breathless and excited, "Every forth wave is bigger. Three small ones and then a bigger one."

"I never noticed that." I say.

"It's true mom." Sarah says as she sits beside me and places her sandy feet on my bare leg.

"Sarah."

Sarah giggles.

"Thanks a lot."

"Now you'll have to come in and wash it off." Sarah says.

"No I wont."

"Why not?"

I grab Sarah and wipe my sand covered leg onto her pant bottom.

"Mom!"

"Now we're even."

Aaron grabs a pile of sand and stands ready to throw it at me.

"Don't you dare throw what's in your right hand."

"Why not?"

"Because you like your allowance too much."

Aaron puts down the sand in his right hand and then picks up a handful with his left and tosses it at my legs.

"I didn't use my right hand." he laughs.

"That's it young man." I laugh, "I got something serious I want to talk about with you two. So I'm gonna let you off this time."

Just then I feel a pile of sand land on the top of my head. I turn around to see Sarah's little hands poised in the air above me.

"Why you little sand monsters."

I grab Sarah and set her into the sand, I place a handful of sand on top of her stomach. Very quickly the three of us are covered in sand. Each of us throwing a handful at a time. Laughing all the way.

"Okay. I give up." I say.

"It's about time. We got you good mom."

"You sure did. Can we talk now?"

"Sure."

The two of them settle down on the sand beside me.

"I've been thinking."

"We know." Aaron says.

"What do you mean 'we know'?"

"Charles told us."

"What did Charles tell you?"

"That we're moving here."

"I didn't tell Charles anything of the sort."

"He just said you really liked it here and that he wouldn't be surprised if you wanted to live here."

"Yeah I guess he did tell you. What do you guys think?"

"Great!"

"Are we going to live with Charles mom?" Sarah asks.

"Only until we get a place of our own."

"I like it here."

"I do too. I'm sure Charles will let us come and visit from time to time, but we've been staying quite a bit with Charles. It's time we give him his life back."

Aaron speaks up, "He said we did give him his life back."

"What did he say?"

"He said we gave him his life back."

"What did he mean by that?"

"I don't know."

"Okay. So you guys don't mind moving to this area?"

Together Aaron and Sarah say, "Cool!"

"Are you guys going to play in the water some more?"

Together they say, "Yes!" and take off running towards the water.

Just then a dog rushes by me sniffing the ground and wagging his tail.

"Hey boy." I say, "Who are you?"

A call from down the beach reaches my ears, "Backwards! Come here boy."

"Is that your name, Backwards?"

Backwards stops and looks at me with his tail waving. Then he gets back to sniffing the ground around me again.

"Backwards. Come here boy." The woman says walking up to us. "I hope he's not bothering you."

Backwards wagging tail hits me in the side of the head. I laugh. "Not at all."

"He just loves the beach."

"Mine too."

"You have a dog?"

"I have a team of terriers." I point to the kids.

"Oh." The woman says and she breaks up laughing. "My name is Marsha."

"Mine's Martha."

"Get out of here."

"Seriously."

"What were our parents thinking?"

"I've asked myself that a couple hundred times."

"Either they did it on purpose to be cruel or they didn't know they were being cruel and were anyway."

"I don't know about that. My name was the same as my grandmother's."

"That's nothing! Mine was on account of the marsh we lived beside at the time."

"I can see why you're disappointed."

"I thought about changing my name for years."

"Why didn't you?"

"I just couldn't be bothered I guess. Not much use in changing once you get used to something."

"That's the best time to change."

"How do you figure that?" Marsha asks.

"Right now is all you've got. All anyone's got really. If you want to change, you're the only one who can do that now."

"You sound like this guy I know at work. He's always talking about life being what you make of it."

"Is he you're boyfriend?"

"Not my type. You might like him though."

"How do you figure that?"

"I just have this feeling."

I smile.

"So what do you say?"

I look into my purse. I find the quarter that Bill gave me so long ago. I look at it and see the message it had for me all along. *In God We Trust.*

"Sure. Why not?"

THE END

AFTER WORD

Life is set up for everyone to win.

Life always matches whatever story you tell with feeling.

If you tell a story of lack and limitation it generally feels bad (not because it is true and reality) rather because it does not look at what the Divine within you knows is possible for you.

Absolutely stop telling stories that do not match what you desire - especially when that reality appears to be in your face - ignore it! If you keep telling any story, you will keep living it.

If you tell a story of abundance and opportunity, it generally feels good (not because it is true and reality YET) rather because is does look at what the Divine within you knows is possible for you. This is a good feeling Creation Vibration Process.

Start telling the best feeling story you can about where you are going and you will get there! When you absolutely know your story is possible, then you will experience it. So start today to tell the best feeling stories about your life and dreams.

By example, if you wish to Tell a Better Feeling Story about Money, one of the ways to do that is to say something like:

I don't have to know the way this is coming to pass. I only have to know with absolute faith that it is coming to pass. There is more money (which is an idea for exchange) available today than at any other time in history. I know that the money I need always comes to me, with time to spare. With this knowledge I relax and feel relief, and because of my relief all goes well for me.

If you wish to Tell a Better Feeling Story about Relationships, one of the ways to do that is to say something like:

I don't have to know the way this is coming to pass. I only have to know with absolute faith that it is coming to pass. There are more loving people available today than at any other time in history. I know that the relationship I desire is as ready for me as I am for it. With this knowledge I relax and feel relief ... and because of my relief, all goes well for me, I meet the right people, I trust life with more hope and belief and my relationships come to me in even better ways than I ever imagined.

When you Trust Life to work out for you, it does.
Barry Thomas Bechta

ACKNOWLEDGEMENTS

I AM Eternally Grateful for God's Presence in my life. My Conscious Unification with each individualisation of God continually transforms my life in extraordinary ways. My world is Now GOD, Greatness Oneness Demonstrated.

I AM grateful to Binah C Godisall for the mirror she is in my life. I wish for her exactly what she wishes for herself as we experience the freedom of Unconditional Love together.

My child like gratitude bubbles forth to Anthony and Zachary. They both have reminded me that it is all just a fun game we are playing together.

Loving thanks to Stephen, Margaret, Gabe, and Sam for all their support as we continue to share our experience.

Warm thanks to my family by blood and by love. My Loving family grows in Oneness each day.

I AM extremely grateful to all the authors that continually inspire me to challenge and expand any limits in my view of God, Love, and Life.

Special Thanks to Richard Bach, Alan Cohen, Robert Kiyosaki, Paulo Coelho, and Ken Blanchard whose works I have throughly enjoyed for their ability to remind me of the Oneness we all are.

Once again thank you to everyone who has ever helped me in any way over the years.

I love all of you very much

ABOUT THE AUTHOR

Barry Thomas Bechta is an artist, author, and film maker whose work centers around the concepts of Unconditional Love. Barry knew he wanted to write from a very young age and was encouraged with his artistic skills and only began writing full time in his thirties. He wrote his first book, *I AM Creating My Own Experience* as a personal journal to choose connection with God/Life/Energy. He has since written 17 inspirational books.

Barry loves to hear from people whom have connected with his writing and used it as a tool to improve their lives. If you would like to write him about your personal experiences as a result of reading any of his books, Barry encourages you to do so.

You can also get a Free Digital Copy of *I AM Creating My Own Experience - The Creation Vibration* from his main website:

www.unconditionallovebooks.com

<u>Unconditional Love Books Titles of Related Interest
by Barry Thomas Bechta</u>

I AM Creating My Own Experience
978-0-9813485-5-1
I AM Creating My Own Answers
978-0-9686835-1-4
I AM Creating My Own Dreams
978-0-9686835-2-1
I AM Creating My Own Relationships
978-0-9686835-3-8
I AM Creating My Own Abundance
978-0-9686835-4-5
I AM Creating My Own Success
978-0-9686835-5-2
I AM Creating My Own Happiness
978-0-9686835-6-9
I AM Creating My Own Experience - The Creation Vibration
978-0-9686835-7-6
I AM Creating My Own Experience - To Manifest Money
978-0-9686835-8-3
I AM Creating My Own Experience - 369 Conscious Days
978-0-9686835-9-0
Loving Oneness
978-0-9813485-0-6
Trust Life
978-0-9813485-1-3
I AM Creating My Own Financial Freedom - The Story
978-0-9813485-2-0
I AM Creating My Own Financial Freedom - The Lessons
978-0-9813485-3-7
Laughing Star's Guide to Laughter, Life, Love, and God
978-0-9813485-4-4

All of the above are books are available through your local
bookstore, or they may be ordered as digital downloads at
www.unconditionallovebooks.com

Barry Thomas Bechta is available for interviews, special events, workshops, and lectures that redefine, guide, and inspire everyone's connection to the Creative Power within themselves. To arrange author interviews, special events, workshops, or lectures, please contact:

UNCONDITIONAL
LOVE BOOKS

Unconditional Love Books
Box # 610 - 2527 Pine St.,
Vancouver, BC, Canada V6J 3E8

info@unconditionallovebooks.com

www.unconditionallovebooks.com

For additional copies of Barry's books, products, and services please contact your local book seller. Many products and services are Only available to order directly from the publisher as eProducts on the website.

Thanks for your purchase and Remember to Consciously Create your Life.

Right Now is the Only Moment of Creation

Enjoy it Fully!

www.ingramcontent.com/pod-product-compliance
Lightning Source LLC
Chambersburg PA
CBHW020639130626
46552CB00003B/1304